Winning!
A Guide To Games That Never Were

Edited by
Brandon Barrows

Published by Raven Warren Studios.
www.ravenwarren.com

Cover art and design by Martin E Brandt II.
Icons made by Lorc, Delapouite, and Faithtoken available on http://games-icons.net

First edition: April, 2016.

Contents

THE HAUTE GAMER'S GUIDE TO THE GURLQUEST
by Carolyn Agee

Picking your Persona: It is well known that the game offers three choices in character creation (aside from alterations in appearance). They are:

Sally - Stay-at-home superwife. Meals are always on the table by the time your husband arrives from work and your home is always immaculate.

Tip: Be prepared for a complete lack of social life and subsequent depression. Alcohol or oxycodone dependency may follow. You are, however, a badass with those scrapbooking scissors.

Partner Happiness: +5, Environment: +5, Self-Realization -1, Weaponry: Scrapbooking scissors.

Chances of husband being stuffed in a refrigerator: 0% (unless you do it yourself). Guard that fridge, girl - you're glued to it already.

#

Hilary - Workplace power player. This choice is a balancing act between the glass ceiling and the expectation that you must sacrifice your love life in order to get ahead.

Tip: Keep an eye on your relational meters. Working late at the exclusion of your love-life does not, in fact, raise your chances of breaking the glass ceiling; as part of your Self-Realization score, you may experience a drop in productivity, leading to an overall downward spiral and ending the game. In order to prevent this, should you find yourself in a depressive state, simply search for the Manic-Pixie Dream-Boy. His zany, uninhibited antics and general lack of agency will boost that happiness meter right up.

Partner Happiness: -2-+4, Environment: +3, Self-Realization +1-+4, Weaponry: The pen is mightier than the sword.

Chances of husband being stuffed in a refrigerator: 60%.

#

Kim - Playing as this persona, you will be more susceptible to societal messages to loathe yourself. This will cause you to spend a disproportionate proportion of your income on creams and cosmetics. Then society will hate you for it. But hey, at least you're well-dressed.

Partner Happiness: +3, Environment: +3, Self-Realization -1, Weaponry: Nail file.

Chances of husband being stuffed in a refrigerator: 60%.

\#

Being Fridged: If you are unfortunate enough to find your husband dismembered and stuffed into your refrigerator, your life goal will be irrevocably altered to "Revenge" and you will transform into Angry Grrrl.

Tip: This is one of the only ways the game allows you to reach full Self-Realization, however, it also allows for total depletion, due to the self being consumed by the life goal.

Partner Happiness: -5, Environment: -5, Self-Realization -5-+5, Weaponry: Anything and everything.

\#

The Hack: In order to circumvent the heteronormative tendencies of the game, there is an unofficial expansion which may be purchased from [website redacted] for $79.99. It must be installed prior to gameplay and includes the following options: Gender modification of sprite, female spousal options, as well as your choice of sexual preference.

The hack will present you with in or out of the closet life paths, both of which have profound implications on Self-Realization and general gameplay. For further information, please see our separate publication, The Gay Bar at the End of the GurlQuest.

\#

Endgame: Remember that the Endgame is to fill all your meters to capacity. As you can see, the game is rigged against you from the outset. Happy questing!

\#

Level One: This level is all about balancing your meters, acquiring as many boosts as possible, and learning to use your weaponry. Although it may seem easy, what you do here has an enormous impact on gameplay. Go into Level Two depleted and the game is lost before it has begun.

You should also engage in social activities outside the home, such as gardening club, happy hour with co-workers, or hanging at the mall in order to build your social network, which will be essential to your success.

Double Boost: If you achieve the near-impossible feat of getting two men to talk to each other about anything other than a woman, you will unlock the much spoken of, but rarely seen, double boost.

#

Level Two: In order to progress to Level Three, you must attain an accolade in your chosen field/hobby. These include, but are not limited to: a professional award (the presentation of which requires you to consume dry chicken in a dimly lit conference room), being voted most popular member of your sorority (which requires vast consumption of cheap alcohol), or the baking semi-finals at the county fair (which requires copious consumption of yummy, yummy cupcakes, to ensure you get the recipe just right).

#

Level Three: At this point in the game, unless he has already been stuffed in a refrigerator, your husband will be kidnapped by someone desiring to win the bakeoff/beauty contest/employee of the month, respectively. Use your social network to search for clues and possible enemies.

Angry Grrrl Mode: If this mode is activated in a prior level, the rest of the game becomes a revenge quest, in which you hunt down and murder the killer, rather than rescue your lover. Basic game play remains the same (though morally questionable), within the confines of the Angry Grrrl persona.

#

Level Four: This is a timed level, as indicated by the uterine shaped hourglass in the upper-right-hand corner. As the sand falls, you will be increasingly accosted by members of your social network, reminding you how little time you have to make little ones. They seem oblivious to the fact that they are actually impeding you from saving the one who would do the inseminating and believe you have simply forgotten this biological imperative.

Please Note: For hack users, this will be changed to "adoption". That's right, QUILTBAG users, even you are not exempt from the societal obsession that you have a child. As soon as possible. Whether you want one or not.

#

Level Five: After defeating hordes all up in your whoha hiatus, you arrive at the unguarded gates. Aided by your nail file/scrapbooking scissors/sword you picked up at the night market and a miraculously appearing coil of super-strength rope, you scale them to find your love unfettered and alone, but you don't have time to question his I.Q. As you've been told (repeatedly), you've got some procreating to do! Just be sure to do it all with the same person, unless, of course, you want to unlock the 'Stoned to Death by the Self-Same Mob of Whoha Stalkers' sequence. All that questing for naught. Such a shame. Then again, we wouldn't have stayed with him, either.

Looney Bin: Levels 1 – 4 Mini-Games
By Brandon Barrows

Overview:

There's plenty of guides out there about how to get through the game's thirty-seven levels, but it seems like most of them ignore what are, in my opinion, the most fun part of all: the mini-games! And Looney Bin has a ton, so you might easily overlook some of the more obscure ones as you navigate the world behind these padded walls, avoiding the likes of professional sadist Nurse Ratchett and finding ways to use Big Elmo's violent tendencies and amorous nature to your advantage.

Since Insanity Points are the currency with which you'll upgrade your various psychoses and physical abilities, and mini-games are a goldmine for collecting them, you'll want to master as many of these fun little diversions as possible. In this guide, I'll show you how to rack up your highest possible score and maximize your enjoyment of life in the Looney Bin!

Level 1:

This, of course, is the "outside level" where you establish what kind of crazy you are and at which institute you'll end up. However, the hospitals are basically all the same in terms of game-play, with only cosmetic differences, so rather than stress about how you'll get into where, take the time to enjoy the mini-games in this area and build a nest-egg of I.P. before ever setting foot in one of the institutions.

Mini-Game #1: Excuse Me, Officer

In the days of yore, this was actually a secret game some of us would play using the various non-player-characters' weird reactions to repetitious stimuli. It was so popular once word got out about it, though, that it's become an official mini-game since the game's second major update roll-out.

The concept of this one is ridiculously simple: when the game starts out and you're free to roam the streets of Sanity City, just find any of the several cops scattered around the various neighborhoods and initiate a dialogue with the conversation button, choose "Excuse me…" as your opener and then, no matter what the N.P.C. does, just keep saying it. It may take a few tries, depending on which cop you pick, but you'll get reactions ranging from a simple brush-off, to a mild insult, to a full-fledged psychotic breakdown, resulting in big point-gains and possibly even meeting your friend in blue in the institute later on. Be careful, though – if you push too hard you can, potentially, quickly end your game by ending up in jail or the morgue, depending on the final result of bugging the cops. The trick is to gauge their reactions and back-off on the conversation for a moment or two if they're getting too worked-up, then resume when you judge it safe to do so. Bonus Tip: If you get the cop to shoot you in the head, there's a small, but completely random, chance that you'll survive. If you do survive, you'll end up with a huge Insanity Point bonus right off the bat. The downside is that it'll affect your motor skills, as well, making some of the game's later levels a lot more challenging.

Mini-Game #2: Watch Me Pee

Easy to learn, difficult to master. The objective of this mini-game is to relieve yourself in public in front of the biggest possible audience with the least possible risk. A lot of people just do it on the street corner, which'll guarantee witnesses in passing cars – who are rather unlikely to do anything about it, of course. That's a safe way to grab a few points, but here's what I like to do: find the Chez Frou-Frou restaurant on 3rd Avenue and wait until about eight p.m. (play a little "Excuse Me, Officer" to pass the time if you haven't already) and just as the restaurant is packed with patrons, walk right up to that big plate-glass window out front and let your golden stream fly. Be sure to make it fast, though, and take off into the alley on the right side of the building, rather than the left. The bus-boys will come out of the kitchen's side-door on the left side of the building and you don't want to make it any easier for them to catch you. If you pull this one off right, you can easily score a wad of I.P. with very little effort.

Level 2:

The first "inside" level, once you've been assigned to a specific "hospital". You'll have to go through some orientation-type stuff and a few therapy sessions before you have a chance to open up any of the mini-games. Those necessaries are boring but I promise it's worth it for the minis.

Mini-Game #1: Let's Rap

This is one of the most-challenging mini-games of the early levels, and probably one of the top three in the entire game, but it's one where you're really free to let your imagination run rampant and use your own creativity to the max, so it's one of my absolute favorites. It's also one that I definitely recommend at least trying out multiple times as it can be difficult to master.

Before unlocking this mini-game, you'll have to complete at least two one-on-one sessions with your assigned doctor, but if you can convince him/her that you're sufficiently well-adjusted socially and would benefit from it (see my walkthrough of the full game for tips), you'll unlock this group-therapy mini-game. Regardless of who your main doctor is, or what institute you're in, your group session's therapist will be "Doctor Kenny", a green-sweater-vest-wearing, white-guy-fro'ed wonder straight out of 1974 – and with therapy skills to match. He's basically one of those feel-good, hippy-with-a-degree-types and the goal of this game is to shock him into silence and end the session. The catch is that the other members of the group will also be trying to shock him and time is limited to forty-five game-minutes (about three real-life minutes), so you have to think fast. Go wild with this one.

Bonus Tip: Doctor Kenny is especially susceptible to shock over sexual stuff. The first time I got maximum points from this mini-game, I told him I wanted to slice off his head, crawl down his neck-hole and make love to him from the inside – all said while wearing my sweetest smile. He ended the session less than two minutes in! Be careful not to make any sort of threats against anyone outside of the facility, though – he'll end the session early, but you'll wind up in lock-down since he'll have evidence you're a danger to society.

Mini-Game #2: Gimme Gimme Shock-Treatment

You can unlock this mini-game only after completing at least four one-on-one sessions with your doctor, which is also the point at which you can move on to level three, so a lot of players miss out on this one. The trick here is to convince the doctor that the drug therapy you're on isn't working and that's actually pretty easy, if you've laid the foundation for the idea that you're a cooperative patient: just don't take the medication they give you. If they think you're serious about getting healthy and can be trusted, they won't check to see if you're cheeking the pills.

Once you've unlocked the shock-treatment mini-game and you're hooked up to the gizmo, it's as easy as can be: just wail on the "B" button as fast as you possibly can to retain consciousness. The longer you stay awake, the more points you'll rake in! All right! If you're very fast on the button and can last long enough, you may even be lucky enough to see smoke pouring out of your ears. Super all right!

Level 3:

While this level takes place outside, in the hospital's recreation yard, it's technically the second "inside" level. It's also the only level that is basically all mini-games, although there's only one that doesn't progress the main storyline (making it the only optional one, basically) so for our purposes, it's the only real mini-game and the only one I'll cover here.

Mini-Game #1: Can I Bum a Smoke?

The easiest mini-game in Looney Bin – just see how many cigarettes you can accumulate by the end of the rec period. Simply walk up to every N.P.C. you can find (it doesn't matter if they're patients or hospital employees) and ask if they can spare a cigarette. It also doesn't matter if they're smoking or not. While you're playing the game, other patients will be, too, so make sure to hit everyone up as quickly as possible. It's only a half Insanity Point per ciggy, but the game's so easy it's basically free points regardless. Bonus Tip: Some N.P.C.s will initially say no or ignore your request, but might give in if asked a second time. This is random as far as I can tell, though, so in the interest of time, don't bother asking the same person twice in a row, just continue making your rounds and if you have time when you're done, go back and hit up the Scrooges again. Also, a warning: you may find someone chewing tobacco, instead of smoking, but don't bug these guys a second time because if they get annoyed, as they'll give you their "leftovers" in a way I promise you won't like.

Level 4:

The return of Doctor Kenny!

Mini-Game #1: Happy Little Trees

Yes, he's back! And this time, the good doctor's taken a cue from his fro'd fellow Bob Ross and leads you in an art-therapy session. Like the last Doctor Kenny mini-game, your objective here is to shock him as much as possible. It's much harder this time around, though, because he's one of those clueless people who thinks all art has inherent value just because it's art, whether it's finger-paints or Fr'angelico. Basically, the bottom line is that you'll have to pull out the big guns here to get significant points.

Bonus Tip: Try extreme violence and/or religious desecration themes here. The sex and vulgarity stuff that worked so well last time is only worth small points here, because the repressed doctor can convince himself that the artistic merits of your work outweigh the shock of boobies and penises openly displayed.

Mini-Game #2: Movie Night
　　　This one is kind of hard. The goal is to be disruptive during the patients' movie night, but make it seem like other patients are the ones causing problems. It's easy enough at the start – just use the "Y" button to crouch down and move along the aisles making noise and throwing things, if you think you can get people's drinks and/or snacks away from them. As the herd thins out, though, you'll find it harder and harder to deflect blame. This is one of the few games where I'd recommend not going for bonus points, just because it's virtually impossible to do. It might be nice to be the only person watching the film, but good luck doing so without getting caught. And if you do get caught, you'll lose movie privileges for a period of time (measured in game-weeks) directly proportionate to how many people you framed. Bonus Tip: Pay attention to who you're framing and try to avoid the violent patients. If you get them kicked out, they'll remember and may well do some kicking of their own the next time you've got outdoor rec period together.
　　　　　　　　　*
Welp, that's all I have time for this time around, fellow Looneys. Seems Doctor Kenny got wind of my ramblings and I've lost internet privileges for… actually, he didn't say how long. Guess I'll have to ask when I see him in group this afternoon. I hope he's forgiven me for Monday's session. Well, lesson learned – dear old Mama Kenny is out of bounds.

At any rate, I hope these little tips prove useful, so until next time, be good, be on the lookout for Ratchett and her rubber hose and maybe I'll see you in the chow-line one of these days.

Fruiternal Quest™
By Russ Bickerstaff

Introduction

Fruiternal Quest™ is something of a semi-forgotten legend
among gamers. There's no record of a game by that name ever
having been released by any company. Nevertheless reports
of its existence have appeared online. The game has even been
put up for sale for various consoles over the years. There's no
question that it does actually exist.

As it has never been formally released, the best guess as to
where it comes from is as strange and idiosyncratic as the
game itself. Any game cartridge, disk or file that goes unused
for long enough, when subject to the right cocktail of heat,
humidity, whimsy and relative proximity to a fruit bowl will
spontaneously mutate into a Fruiternal Quest™ game.

As it has never been formally released, there has never been
an instruction booklet discovered for the game. Some
relatively fundamental aspects of Fruiternal Quest™ vary
from console to console, game to game and moment to
moment. This situation makes a detailed strategy guide
almost impossible. The somewhat erratic foundations of the
game have caused many to lose interest out of sheer
frustration. Too often these games have been discovered,
discarded and dismissed as a strange, little fantastically
elaborate glitches.

　　　What this text will attempt to do is define the basics of
the game in hopes that those who encounter it in the future
will be able to better appreciate the beauty of what is surely
the most pleasantly enigmatic puzzle ever to have evolved in
the history of software.

Main Menu Screen
Once Fruiternal Quest™ has been booted-up, the logo of the game appears above its hero: the Strawberry Banana Gnome. (SBG.) He appears in absurdly high-resolution regardless of the platform he's inhabiting, which can be kind of difficult to get used to. He's standing there patiently waiting for the game to start next to a window with start-up options. Long, vertically oriented black eyes occasionally blink on a khaki oval noseless background over a fuzzy, mouthless white beard on chubby, little yellow body with featureless yellow arms and legs nubs. (No feet or hands.) His little, yellow body tapers off into a little, yellow head, tapering off into a little, yellow point. A pair of long, strawberry tassels originate from the pointy tip of his yellow head and hang down to his little arm nubs. He glances around waiting for things to get going. There have been some reports of the little guy doing whimsical things on that main screen. He has been known to hop around playfully engaging in those looking-in on him when babies, toddlers and pets are in the same room as the game console, but these are largely unsubstantiated claims.

Getting to Know the Gnome
When gameplay is engaged, the fruity side-scrolling environment of Fruiternity appears. The background varies with the game and the time of day. Usually there is a lemony sun high in the sky. There are mountains and valleys of various fruits in the background and foreground. There on the lower left side of the screen is the Strawberry Banana Gnome. He is intently looking around the environment, perhaps stretching a bit if it's been a particularly long time since the game was last booted-up.

The game's interface is fairly straightforward. A joystick or directional pad will seem to move SBG in one of four different directions. The rest of the buttons vary. The button closest to the directional pad is usually the jump button. There is another button somewhere on any control pad that allows the strawberry tassels to be whipped back and forth. A third button (or a combination between the directional and the first two) has been known to allow the gnome to have a conversation with the two strawberries that are his little, red tassels. The gnome and the two strawberries will whisper inaudibly to each other for a few minutes. The gnome will occasionally look back at the screen to see that you're still there and then go back to the conversation. This has been known to last quite some time. It is uncertain whether or not these conversations have any effect on gameplay at all. Strawberry-based flight is a little-known ability. Press the strawberry tassel button fast enough or in some combination of motions with the directional pad and the strawberry tassels begin to spin faster and faster until SBG lifts up off the ground. From there, the directional pad will allow the gnome to move freely in any direction at all through the air. A ceiling has never been discovered to the upper atmosphere of Fruiternity. Get high enough up and the little gnome starts to get dizzy. Be careful: he has been known to falter and fall to the ground with a haphazard bounce.

A Few Words About the Control Pad

It should be pointed out that the control pad does not actually control the gnome. It's helpful to think of the control pad as your way of communicating with SBG. Your use of the control pad is your way of suggesting actions that he might take. He sometimes hesitates when prompted in one direction or another. Sometimes he gets distracted and decides to have a conversation with a passing fruit that has nothing to do with the game at all. When danger presents itself, he can be quite stubborn. Say for instance that you prompt him to walk off a cliff into a pit filled with angry, sinister, little breakfast pastry goblins. He'll turn to face the screen, look straight at you and firmly shake his little head. The more insistent you become, the more insistent he becomes. Be prepared: this can turn into a test of wills that you may not win.

SBG has been known to spot something off-screen and wave hello to it. He'll face the screen, motion you to wait and put the game on pause while he walks out of view. You are left holding the controller in front of a motionless screen while the pleasantly whimsical environmental sounds of Fruiternity play on. Listen closely and you may hear whispers and staticky laughter. Be patient. It has been known to take up to a half hour for him to return. Gameplay then resumes as normal.

Engaging the Environment

The land of Fruiternity is a strange and whimsical place. There is very little that you can't climb on, walk on, eat or have a casual conversation with. With no scores or achievements to unlock and nothing else to denote any kind of actual progress during the game, some have begun to wonder if it was ever meant to have any discernible goal at all. Many a gamer has watched the lemony sun sink into the distant horizon in bemused silence before reluctantly calling it a day.

Rest assured there is, in fact, some sort of ultimate goal (usually). There is no set pattern for gameplay, however, and there have been as many different plots and goals reported as there are copies of the game and people playing them. Every time one of these games appears another story is discovered with a completely new goal and a completely different strategy of how to achieve it.

The important thing when trying to discover the goal of the game is to be at least half as whimsical as it is. Meaning and significance can be found in the strangest places. Strike up a conversation with a few grapes if you're stuck. (Grapes are notoriously chatty, but after an hour or so, they might tell you some juicy rumors.) Rumors become clues. Clues become mini-quests. Before long you may find yourself entrenched in the slimy, doughy corridors in the halls of the breakfast pastry goblins. You may find yourself discussing politics and philosophy with a pineapple or perhaps saving a family of lychees from a runaway tide of chocolate syrup.

Somewhere along the line, the plot begins to present itself. It follows a pretty intelligible line even if it seems to be inundated with dead-ends and non-sequiturs. By the time you have played enough to discover the rhythm of the plot, you develop a kind of a dialogue with the game. There's a synthesis between player, gnome and game environment that can play strange tricks with time. You may have been playing the game for hours, days, weeks, months or even years, but by the time the plot has reached its conclusion, any player feels as though the whole thing was perhaps over before it started.

Once a game of Fruiternal Quest™ has been played to its inevitable conclusion, the game returns to what it had been prior to the mutation without any real indication that it had ever been anything other than what it was prior to the transformation. There have, however, been fleetingly sparse sightings of anomalies on the games that had previously hosted Fruiternal Quest™. Look closely around the edges of gameplay and you might see a pair of blinking black eyes above a fuzzy white beard somewhere in the background. By the time you've fully taken stock of what you're looking at, it will vanish in the sound of staticky laughter.

Much of the rest of the lore surrounding Fruiternal Quest™ is anecdotal and unsubstantiated. Those coming to this text looking for more explicit strategy may be a bit upset with it. More detailed strategies are available elsewhere, but they tend to read more like personal journals and travelogues of Fruiternity than anything that could possibly be of much use in a strategic capacity. A chance encounter with Fruiternal Quest™ can be an amazing thing. The important thing is not to get frustrated. If you're lucky enough to have run into this game, there are some really great opportunities here. The important thing is to be open to anything the game throws at you. Just try not to take it too seriously.

Buffet Hero
By Eric Hawthorn

Press Start to begin Level One. A very skinny Hungry Pete
enters Angelo's Pizzeria, Home of the State's Largest Pizza
Buffet!

It's time to put Angelo out of business.

Press A to eat the pizzas: cheese, extra cheese,
pepperoni, sausage, meat-lover's, Hawaiian. Enjoy the pasta,
heaped with grated cheese. Slurp up the chicken and veal and
eggplant parmigiana. Swallow fistfuls of meatballs and greasy
breadsticks and drink marinara sauce straight from its ladle.
Thirsty? Hungry Pete can stick his head under the soda
fountains and drink directly from the nozzle. Drink regular
cola, not diet.

→ Fun Fact: Buffet Hero's creators originally wanted to
call the game Food Orgy.

Perhaps you're beginning to feel full. This is because of
the console add-ons included with this game, which are
responsible for the taste and fullness sensations that make
Buffet Hero the most realistic binge-eating simulator ever
created.
A few words about these accessories:

The Hunger Helmet sends gentle shocks to the brain's
hypothalamus, controlling the sensation of fullness. The
Hunger Helmet's electrodes alternately stimulate and inhibit
the brain's recognition of satiety. When Hungry Pete is
hungry, the gamer is hungry. When Hungry Pete is full, the
gamer is full. Thus we see the central challenge of Buffet Hero:
to override the biological sensation that says "Stop eating!" To
succeed in this game, Hungry Pete must never stop eating.

→ Pro Tip: Keep an extra set of batteries on hand
during extended gaming sessions. The Hunger Helmet uses a
lot of juice.

The Flavor Generator fits like an orthodontic retainer on the roof of the mouth and emits taste chemicals during gameplay to create the fullest possible experience of compulsive eating. If Hungry Pete inhales a slice of triple-cheese pizza, the gamer gets to enjoy the taste of triple-cheese pizza. If Hungry Pete consumes a piece of broccoli — something to avoid — the player will unfortunately experience this as well.

→ Caution: Do not eat actual food during gameplay. This may damage the Flavor Generator, leading to inaccurate tastes and an unenjoyable gaming experience.

Let's return to Angelo's Pizzeria.

At this point, Hungry Pete feels pretty sluggish from all the carbs. The player is likewise ready for a nap, having vicariously consumed many thousands of calories. Remember this is a simulation of extreme fullness; you feel bloated because Hungry Pete is bloated.

On to the dessert table! Help yourself to the éclairs and ice cream and cookies until —

"Not-a so fast!" cries Chef Angelo, bursting from the kitchen with a gleaming pizza cutter. He's followed by various white-aproned kitchen staff brandishing knives and pots and pans.

Cycle through your weapons by holding down the B button and pressing Up. In Level One, Hungry Pete is poorly armed: he has a fork, a spoon, and a lunch tray. Your best bet is the lunch tray, which allows you to dispatch your opponents from a safe distance. Since Chef Angelo is only a Level One boss, you won't find him too difficult. This early in the game, Hungry Pete is still quite nimble. Once you've defeated Angelo and his kitchen goons, you can exit the level.

This brings you to the Doctor's Office for Hungry Peter's between-level weigh-in. Our hero stands in his underwear on a rotating scale while the game tallies his progress in calories. This early in the game, Hungry Pete's ribs are still somewhat visible, his knees jutting from skinny legs. But he's clearly gained some weight since beginning his mission of non-stop consumption: he is cultivating a paunch and chest-area flabbiness and his butt is in expansion mode. Not bad for one level!

→ Note: The greater one's success, the fatter Hungry Pete gets.

Level Two: Start by crossing the strip mall's parking lot to enter King Kong Buffet, a massive Asian buffet staffed by deadly ninjas. A poster on the door features a picture of you, Hungry Pete, and the words Banned from Area Restaurants!

Disregard this sign.

Notice it's Early Bird Special time at King Kong Buffet; there is an army of senior citizens in the dining area. An inexperienced gamer may wish to avoid confrontation with these elderly diners and wait patiently in line at the various buffet tables. But your fiercely grumbling stomach will remind you of your calling: non-stop caloric intake. Because of your Hunger Helmet, waiting in line is an agonizing process.

Do what you have to do is the point.

→ Pro Tip: A senior citizen's walker makes an excellent weapon once the tennis balls are pulled off the legs. Get a cane, too. You'll need the cane in future levels, when Hungry Pete has become too fat to stand on his own.

Once you've cleared the area of senior citizens, venture over to the salad bar. The salad bar is a dangerous area populated by menacing wait-staff who throw ninja stars. Even worse, they hurl vegetables like nutritious grenades. You must dodge flying broccoli, heads of lettuce, and celery stalks. Though the broccoli is calorie-neutral and only slows your progress, the lettuce and celery actually subtract calories from your total. Avoid these dangerous foods.

Visit King Kong Buffet's fried-foods table. Here is where you'll find the egg-rolls and fried chicken and French fries and soggy, Asian-buffet-style pizza. Everything is a different shade of yellow. This is a great place to practice more advanced eating techniques:

• The Shovel: Hold down the Forward button and double-tap A to lift an entire tray-load of food and pour it into Hungry Pete's mouth.

• The Juggler: Hungry Pete uses alternating hands to toss pieces of food into his mouth. This can be done extremely quickly and is best when running low on time.

• Finally, let's practice The Whale, in which Hungry Pete belly-slides across a buffet table, mouth open wide, and takes everything into his mouth, sans chewing, like a whale sucking in plankton.

→ Fun Fact: Compulsive overeating is a psychological disorder afflicting millions of Americans. This behavior can lead to hypertension, heart disease, and diabetes.

Visit the dessert table, where you will find cockroaches crawling among the dessert items. Don't worry, the cockroaches are harmless, simply there to add authenticity to this $7.99 strip mall buffet. Try the strawberry cheesecake and the triple fudge brownies. The cockroaches are edible, too, for what it's worth.

The stir-fry table in the next room is where you will face the level's boss, a masked stir-fry chef. Load a pile of raw pork onto a plate and have the chef heat it in a syrupy sauce, which will double the caloric value. The catch is you must battle the stir fry chef while the food is being cooked. The chef will throw hot morsels of meat at you and attempt to knock you on the head with his shovel-like spatula as other ninja wait-staff, armed with nunchuks and throwing stars, converge on your location.

→ Pro Tip: Fight off your attackers by throwing plates.

Back to the Doctor's Office! A chart on the wall suggests Hungry Pete is borderline diabetic. His paunch is now a gut that hangs in tiers like a curtain at the opera. His legs disappear into shadow beneath his impressively amorphous derriere, which absorbs his underwear like pre-solidified Jell-O. Hungry Pete has a double chin and the wrinkled corpulence of nature's largest manatees. Progress!

→ Pro Tip: Take a moment to remove your electrode headgear and walk around. Maybe go outside for a few minutes. Occasional breaks are necessary to prevent fatigue, muscle stiffness, and psychological dependence. Buffet Hero can be addictive.

When Hungry Pete gets home, his uniformly skinny extended family is waiting in the living room. This is an intervention.

Thus begins one of the longer cut-scenes in the game. Relatives crowd the sofa and chairs from the dining room and tell Hungry Pete how worried they are for his health. Someone reads a poem. Hungry Pete blankly nods.

Throughout this challenging level, there is one thing to keep in mind: these people want to take away your food. Hungry Pete must reach the Refrigerator as quickly as possible while his skinny supposed-loved ones give chase and throw cauliflower and celery stalks at him, blathering about their feelings vis-à-vis Hungry Pete's way-serious eating disorder.

→ Note: In addition to throwing icky vegetables, they may also hurl bottles of syrup of ipecac. Vomiting can be useful when overrun by attacking relatives – vomiting in their faces temporarily blinds them, giving Hungry Pete the opportunity to waddle away and regroup. But Hungry Pete's caloric score is negatively impacted each time he vomits. Barf judiciously.

Hungry Pete does in fact have an ally in this stage: Hungry Sam, his morbidly obese dachshund that pushes itself around on what might, beneath all the rolls of canine fat, be a skate board. Hungry Sam is a helpful sidekick: you can push him into approaching assailants to slow them down and bite at their ankles. Despite his corpulence, Hungry Sam somehow manages to stay with you all the way to the Refrigerator, at which point — provided all the enemies overrunning your house have been dispatched — Hungry Sam will beg for food. If you refuse to feed Hungry Sam, he will bite you.

→ Pro Tip: Kill Hungry Sam.

At the Doctor's Office, Hungry Pete's underwear is invisible beneath his sagging gut and back fat. His feet are puny, his hands tiny disappointments at the ends of swollen sausage arms. Hungry Pete is red-faced and lathered with sweat from the exertion of his recently completed level. His breathing is quite audible from this point forward (a nice touch on the part of the game's sound effects people).

On the way into his next restaurant, Hungry Pete sees a community bulletin-board. Stop and pull off one of the bulletins: a flyer for a Japanese hotdog eating competition. Why a Japanese hotdog eating competition would advertise on an American bulletin board is anyone's guess; we'll need to forgive the game's narrative laziness here and just suspend our disbelief.

As our hero wheezes his way into Sal's Seaside Seafood, the player would be wise to make use of the cane he procured earlier at the King Kong Buffet. (See? There's a reason we had you rob an elderly person!). While Hungry Pete won't travel as quickly as he did in Level One, the cane reduces his need to sit down and catch his breath.

Sal's Seaside Seafood is a greasy, sprawling complex of cracking shells and tearing flesh crowded with people who share Hungry Pete's predilection. Notice an overhead banner that says Welcome International Dieticians' Convention.

First, Hungry Pete must compete with his greasy fellow diners, who for reasons unknown throw both cooked and live shellfish at him. This is a unique dynamic, both advantageous and threatening. After all, these crabs and lobsters and clams are rich in calories and ideal for Hungry Pete's purposes, but hurled as weapons can severely injure him (particularly when they hit him in the face). On the first table of the restaurant is a gleaming shell-cracker. This tool is essential: the gamer must use the cracker to split open the flying shellfish as they sail through the air. Once cracked open, these shellfish are a tasty treat (especially for gamers who are allergic to seafood and wouldn't have the opportunity to taste it any other time).

→ Fun Fact: Lobsters and crabs are boiled alive. Their screaming is actually the sound of air hissing from their exoskeletons, not actual screaming.

Fortunately, Hungry Pete has allies here. The kids at the long lobster-evisceration tables use slingshots to send morsels of delicious crab and lobster meat in quick greasy arcs across the restaurant's aisles. You can catch these morsels in your mouth as you attempt to deflect and crack open the buttery crustaceans hurled your way by the more hostile older diners. Remember, don't hurt the kids. The kids are your friends.

→ Fun Fact: Obesity affects approximately one-third of America's children.

Then we have the dieticians congregated at the end of the dining room. The dieticians are armed to the teeth with celery and Brussels sprouts and ipecac. These white-coated professionals are lean and nimble and extremely hostile. Of the many points in the game where death is imminent, few compare to Hungry Pete's encounter with the dieticians.

Next, the player must battle the hulking, tank-top wearing grease-ball known as Sal. He stands behind a roiling lobster tank and throws live lobsters at you. One cannot defeat Sal. The player must simply stay alive long enough — dodging airborne snapping lobsters, cracking open the occasional lobster for consumption — until the police arrive.

Yes, the police.

At this point in the game, Hungry Pete has no neck. His eyes and mouth are tiny holes poked into a red bloated pie of a face. The most noticeable change since the last weigh-in is his belly's new consistency. What was once a single solid gut, albeit one with a few overlapping ranges of fat, is now a soft, hairy expanse. It is a rippling ocean of fat, this belly, this gut, the sort you can lean close to and blow on and watch the fat ripple away. You can skip rocks across this fat, stick your arm deep into this fat, perhaps put on some swimming trunks and go for a relaxing swim in this tidal outpouring of fat. Hungry Pete is not simply a person who is fat but fat that is also a person. Fat fat.

He is also in jail.

The prison level adds a new tension to Hungry Pete's mission of reckless consumption. Hungry Pete must eat constantly even in this place of scarcity. Meals are limited to a plop of this, a slice of that, and maybe a small bowl of tinny fruit cocktail on the side. Prison is a place of desperate privation, as far as Hungry Pete is concerned. Getting more food will take creativity.

Press Start to check your inventory. Your previous arsenal of weapons (pizza cutter, cane, fork and knife, etc.) has been confiscated, but somehow Hungry Pete has gotten his fat sweaty mitts on a good old-fashioned prison shank.

→ Pro Tip: If you want to eat, you need to stab somebody.

The individual cells are open during the day, so Hungry Pete can squeeze out and join the other inmates in line for grub. The cafeteria is a big, open space with metal-caged lights and some clearly established table assignments. Over here we have the Mexican gangsters. Over here are the bikers. Over here a gang of meth-addled Aryan Nation boys. Etcetera.

If you want, you can wait in line for one measly serving of food. Or you can start a prison-wide riot and sneak away to eat every bit of food behind the cafeteria counter.

You need to shank just the right person. We recommend stabbing one of the Aryan Nation guys, which will trigger a fight with the adjacent Mexicans, the fight spilling over into the rest of the prison cafeteria. Lumber away as fast as possible so as not to be pulled into the fight.

Have you stabbed your tweaker white supremacist yet? Great! Let's eat.

The charges against Hungry Pete, whatever they were, are dropped. Freed from jail, our hero goes international.

This happens because of the advertisement Hungry Pete found earlier – the incongruous flyer advertising a hotdog eating competition in Japan. Next thing we know he's squeezing into a plane bound for Tokyo. In this extended cut-scene, we follow the jet's path from America across the Atlantic. In reality, most flights from the U.S. to Japan travel west rather than east, a fact we will have to ignore because the flight's eastward trajectory is essential to what happens next: due to an unusually heavy passenger, the plane experiences mechanical problems and is forced to make an emergency landing in war-torn Somalia!

Hungry Pete finds himself on the dusty streets of a sub-Saharan tent city, a starving waste-scape of tattered canvas and sun-charred vegetation. The only way Hungry Pete can eat is if he makes it to the most important establishment in this godforsaken place: the Red Cross tent at the center of the camp.

The villagers are dark and skeletal, with sunken eyes and jutting cheekbones. They lean against ropy palm trees and stare at you, or stare at the ground, or tend to their listless children sitting in the dust. Ignore the big-eyed starving faces peering at you from the edges of the cracked-dirt street. These people live each day in a shriveled agony that you, a phenomenally obese American, can't possibly understand.

→ Pro Tip: To hell with them. You need to eat.

This level is arguably one of the toughest in the game, since there is no buffet at all. A stark contrast to previous stages, this Somalian refugee village is a place where starving hordes fight one another for access to gray-wrapped food bars distributed at the Red Cross tent.

→ Note: Many of the villagers are armed with AK-47s. Do not underestimate the refugees vying for these food bars.

There is a no shortage of hungry refugees who will battle you for food. Stay on your guard, even while eating. If you manage to wrest an AK-47 from one of the more dangerous refugees, mowing everybody down will buy you a few minutes of undisturbed gorging time before another wave of hungry villagers — better armed this time — converges on your position.

Kudos! Few but Hungry Pete could successfully gain weight in a Somalian refugee camp. At this point, Hungry Pete is a complex wave pool of overlapping, undulating flesh. His arms no longer rest at his sides but are pushed outward by underarm fat to flap like baby arms. There is absolutely no evidence of existing genitals.

Unfortunately, the Somalian refugee camp is not the last obstacle between Hungry Pete and his hotdog eating competition. Though his plane is repaired and returned to the air, its mechanical soundness is short-lived: something goes terribly wrong once more as the plane passes over the Himalayas. The plane's lights flicker and cabin rocks about. Then the windows shatter and are sucked from the plane and the oxygen masks drop from above. Soon, the sides of the plane rip open and pieces of wing spin through the cabin, severing passengers' limbs and heads while Hungry Pete, munching on a pack of airline peanuts, unused oxygen mask bouncing above his head, turns blue. The shredded cabin shakes violently. With a deafening crash, the screen goes dark.

Brightness. Snow everywhere. Smoky pieces of wreckage. Distant screams. Hungry Pete appears unharmed until the player attempts to move or looks down: no legs.

He is a blob of fat wearing an undersized coat in a spreading expanse of red snow.

→ Fun Fact: His legs were a lost cause anyway. If the plane wreck hadn't taken them, diabetes would have.

Thus begins the plane wreck level, taking the previous stage's challenge of scarcity and compounding this problem with the fact that Hungry Pete can no longer stand. Now, he must drag himself through the snow, leaving a slug trail of red in his wake. The crash site is an expanse of blood- and grease-streaked snow littered with pieces of the plane and its passengers. There are occasional survivors among the wreckage, in varying degrees of dismemberment, crawling through the snow and attempting to patch themselves up.

Before you can eat you must deal with the challenge of moving around. Notice you're within arm's reach of someone's leg (one of yours? No). Use this leg as a sort of prop or cane to push and drag yourself through the snow until you reach a relatively large suitcase. Struggle onto this suitcase and use it to slide along the surface of the snow without sinking. Continue to push yourself along with the leg. Listen for avalanches.

Abominable snowmen, those mythical, furry creatures said to exist in the mountains of Tibet and Nepal, will arrive to feed on the pieces of human flesh scattered about the debris field. They will also attempt to eat you.

→ Pro Tip: Fight them off with the leg.

True, Hungry Pete's plane has crashed in the yeti-infested Himalayas, but this does not mean he is off the hook when it comes to his mission of absolute gluttony. Hungry Pete must eat. The crash site does indeed, as the abominable snowmen demonstrate, offer some amount of edible material – if one is open-minded. There is no time for vacillation or moral deliberation. Hungry Pete must act. (An inexperienced buffet hero may be tempted to remove the Flavor Generator before the feasting begins. This isn't necessary; the taste isn't half bad.)

→ Pro Tip: You know what you have to do.

Hungry Pete's leg stumps are bandaged. The rest of him is fatter than ever. Hungry Pete is less a distinct entity than a general mass of bodily abstractions – waves and flaps, indents and crevices. His eyes are tiny squints beneath an overhang of forehead. The blood running down his face and chest has been scrubbed away, all evidence of the previous level's unpleasantness—leg stumps notwithstanding—cleaned up.

The game culminates with the International Hotdog Eating Championship in Tokyo. The surrounding stadium is white and gold. The sky is blue, the tablecloth before Hungry Pete a creamy white.

→ Fun Fact: How did Hungry Pete get here? In the previous level, he was bleeding and freezing to death on a mountaintop. And now he is in a Japanese hotdog eating contest?

The competitors consist of some fat Hawaiian guy, a skinny Asian woman, and Hungry Sam, Hungry Pete's deceased former pet.

→ Note: What? If Hungry Sam is here, what does this say about Hungry Pete's condition? Perhaps he isn't in Tokyo after all...

When the official fires his gun, hotdogs begin raining from the sky and plopping on the table before Hungry Pete and his competitors. Some of the hotdogs are in buns, some are not. There are cheese dogs and chili dogs and corn dogs and pizza dogs. The stadium is raining ketchup and mustard and hot sauce and relish and nacho cheese!

→ Pro Tip: Pick up your pace! The skinny Asian woman is leading the way. You must execute pretty fancy combo moves (two or three hotdogs at a time) if you want to overtake her.

The hotdogs are delicious. Plump and savory, not too salty. They get juicier with every bite. You could eat these hotdogs all day, but hurry! The clock is ticking! You're so close to winning the game! So close you can taste it.

When you do win, if you win, the game simply fades to white.

→ Note: Once the game has concluded, you may be tempted to restart your system and immediately replay Buffet Hero. This game is as addictive as its delicious foods. We advise you to take a break before replaying. Take five. Go on a walk, get some fresh air. Remove the game's headset and taste implant. Go relax.

In fact, go have a snack. Seriously, when was the last time you ate?

You must be starving.

Winning at Hedgehog Card Party 2 – The Final Mini-Games
by Jose Cardoso

Hedgehog Card Party 2 is the much-anticipated sequel to
Hedgehog Card Party, featuring enormous variety with over
fifteen boards and two-hundred mini-games! Take that,
Plumber Party.
This guide details strategies on the concluding mini-games for
each map, while a future installment will cover an overview of
the boards themselves, followed by full breakdowns of the
standard mini-games in the final part of this three-part series.
Let's get shuffling!

#

Prison Break
Map: Scorched Mountain
Nothing spells inescapable doom like a prison inside a
volcano. But today, you will break free--or break something.
Keep up with your post of feeding chili to prisoners as tthey
walk down the line, using the analog stick to stir and the A
button to pour. When the guards turn their backs, add red
peppers and hot sauce with the B button to crank the heat up
as fellow prisoners wait with an expression of combined
confusion and acceptance. As the guards prepare to turn back
around, return to your post or risk immediate disqualification.
Keep this up until 2:00, then from 2:00 to 3:00 will be the
second phase: players leap over the counter and start lobbing
chili everywhere. Your effectiveness in the first phase will
determine how quickly items will burn, meaning a slow burn
for points without a scalding recipe. Aim for the tables since
they have the most real estate, as does the kitchen in the back.

Jungle Book-It
Map: Tit Tat Ruins
Everyone starts off in the same area on their own rail, but the very first bend will separate the four players into pairs that follow along the left and right of the jungle. From then on, you'll need to start switching rails with the analog stick to avoid hitting the tree branches. Hold down the B button to accelerate, but be sure to slow down before the giant raindrops fall or you'll slip through the rail with them. Focus on the rail of your colour so as not to confuse your character with someone else's as the pairs get shuffled in the middle. All four rails converge eventually, followed by a final climb to the temple eye. Use the A button to jump to a block, or perform a double-jump if you're feeling confident about reaching two ahead of you. If you mess up on timing, you'll slip through the gaps and have to start again so don't get cocky.

Garg Oil
Map: Divine Garden
The flying mantas are unable to fire repeated attacks willy-nilly, so be conservative over ammo or you'll need to head for resting stations to reload. Gargoyles only stand in place for a few moments before taking off again, so that's your opportunity for a long-range attack using the A button. Make sure not to trail too close behind any of the flying gargoyles or they'll spew oil, rendering you immobile for a few seconds. The airborne gargoyles award more points than those situated closer to the ground, but their erratic flight patterns make them harder to strike. Also be on the lookout for pesky rivals chasing the same creature. Drop an oil-bomb to stun them for two seconds, but remember the reverse applies too!

Wispy Warmongers
Map: Planet Lisp
Winning strategies are those focused on mass destruction versus constant pelleting. Move through the winding course in search of the planet's lisp-talking inhabitants. Build an army — say about fifty or so — then return to the start to deploy them from the cannon pointed at the construction site. The challenge of creating a crash site is that the cannon is shared between all players, hence you may be tempted to take a gradual approach. But the key is to be the last blast that will destroy the structure, so keep fifty creatures on hand for when its health hits about 35% for a finishing move. At any point, you can exchange twenty-five creatures to put all rivals to sleep for five seconds, but don't overdo it.

Ack, Relics!
Map: Ghastly Chambers
The north chamber presents the best opportunity to force an early elimination. After retrieving a relic and a mud bomb, head into the chamber and purposely activate the mystery jewel, which will cause you to drop all items. Leave the items on the ground and make your way back out to have the doors close behind you. Once the ghosts start picking off defenseless treasure hunters, any unsuspecting opponents who desperately race for the relic you dropped will also trigger the mud bomb, preventing them from leaving the chamber without someone tripping the hourglass from outside. This sorry state of affairs will leave them even more vulnerable than before, for now they have nowhere to hide after their relic is destroyed from deflecting one of the several roaming ghosts. Ace relics.

Broke-Back Countin'
Map: Oceanstate Palace
The giant turtles that pass through the current are usually an impressive bunch, but every once in a while some put on more than they can carry. Monitor the flow of turtles outside the palace, keeping mental count of those whose backs give out. When they do, everything on them will fall into the ocean, creating an isolated whirlpool that pulls other turtles in, sometimes causing their backs to give out as well in the chaos. Turtles caught in the whirlpool spin around four times before disappearing, so count their rotations as other whirlpools are created elsewhere. Closest tally wins.

Brinking Sands
Map: Itchy-Eyes Desert
Everyone starts at the top of the quicksand pit, but to be the last player with their head above sand, hurl insults at rivals to lower their resistance levels and make them sink faster. Selectively choose words from the chimps as they swing from one side of the screen to the other. Targeting a specific rival for the moment produces the best results, so watch for their resistance levels to dip before launching a tirade of phrases like "faker" and "giant talking egg." At the same time, balance out attacks with resistance-building words and phrases like "just smile" and "damn, not here." Remember to keep mashing the A button to keep your resistance levels up.

Casino Ark
Map: Disco Highway
The epicenter for fast-money activity, Casino Ark is a secret codename given by the "underground" leaders to conceal the true mystery of the otherwise inconspicuous satellite known as... The Inconspicuous Satellite. Lurk close to slot players and wait for them to do a victory dance, then retrieve any chips dropped by them. Don't get too close or security will send you to the jail on the top floor. Although this floor doesn't feature chips, there are slides at the north-east and south-west corners that lead to the bottom floor. Activating the ball drop will allow you to make use of these to knock rivals, but also follow behind so you can retrieve dropped loot. If the alarm sounds, rush to one of three elevators while the slot players hide from nosy astronauts peering in from the outside. If you don't make it in time, you'll lose all your chips, so use the B button to punch rivals out of the way. Note that not all slot players will end up winning, nor will successive plays have identical winners.

Shipwreck Sabotage
Map: Pillaged Seas
The only way out of this sunken ship is to tickle the octopus at its pores, but you can't do that with the scuba gear you have on. Use what's around you to destroy your suit and rupture its sensitive spot. Bumping into rivals is the slowest way to reduce your armour, plus the collision will send you spinning upward. Similarly weak is rubbing your armour between the treasure chests at the bottom. Near there, however, are two giant clams. Wedge yourself into the opening as it closes and the pressure will do considerable damage, but the full effect takes 10 seconds. Each clam will only attack once for the whole game, so use them right away or save them for your last move. Another option is to stay by the small window towards the stern: a shark will occasionally poke its head through with a slightly open mouth, allowing you to scrape your armor against its teeth. Be sure to pull away before it snaps back, or the attack will damage more than your suit. Open the door to the captain's quarters to send jellyfish floating upward and stun rivals. With them gone, you'll find mines that can be set to explode after five seconds, but bring them to an isolated area or you'll help your rivals.

Dawn of the Doomed
Map: Doom's Aplomb
Search the rooms in the facility while keeping your energy up to be the last one standing. Prolong your patience levels as long as you can by finding one of the thirty-five experiments to bring your energy level up by ten points of the total ten. The longer the game goes, the fewer points you'll earn for finding an experiment. A maximum of five experiments will appear at any given time, and the locations and point values will refresh every thirty seconds. If you discover the location of an experiment when you have full energy, you may want to commit this room to memory and return a few seconds later when you have less energy. Refer to the map and head in the direction of your rivals to divert attention from the area. Alternatively, locate a bomb generator so you can plant one in the room where an experiment is hiding. Be sure not to trigger it yourself later on or you'll lose hefty points.

Crash-Test Homey
Map: Orca Stroll
The young fox has become savvy to the fact that he's often without a rescuer whenever he crashes his plane, hence the inane training exercise. Whip out your bazookas and shoot down the fox dolls as they pilot toy planes across the sky, then catch them as they spin out of control before they fall to the ground. Be sure not to catch the same one you shot down or you'll lose points (better than having to explain yourself for fabricating danger!). Most hero points wins.

Mind My Step
Map: Izina Crisis
Work with your partner to herd a gullible silver droid to your side of the arena. For the first part, the two on the field lay two traps on the opposing team's side. If the droid trips over one, it will reset to its starting position and lose a life. It's best to position most traps near the center of the path, which will force resets more often in the struggle. Subsequently, the other two stationed at machines must taunt the droid to their zone, repeatedly yelling "I'm the trigger" in different directions using the analog stick. Once it crosses, it'll be trapped by the mind control field and be forced to attack the other team, bringing them down a life point and ending the round. The game will end once two life points are lost by either team, or when the droid loses five lives –
whichever happens first.

Haunted Man Shun
Map: Hassle Castle
Someone's been spending too much time with the pumpkin-headed ghosts. Use the fixtures in the mansion's courtyard to dodge the eerie creatures for as long as possible. As the game progresses, more will join, always entering from the east and west gates. Every ten-second interval for the first thirty seconds, a carving tool will appear at the north courtyard gate, allowing you protect yourself from a single attack. There's no rule against one player picking up all three, provided that they have a vacant slot. Thus, with a tool in your possession, purposely get hit by a creature as the ten-second mark approaches so you can retrieve the item as it re-appears. With this strategy, you can force a more difficult game upon your rivals.

My Jewels Lie Over the Canyon
Map: Rockick Valley
Work as a team to draw the red droid away from its private
jewel stash, then have your partner go after the treasure. You
can take multiple jewels at once, but these will need to be
carried back to your base; and the more in your hand, the
slower you'll become. Note that distracting the droid will also
leave its jewels open for the opposing team, so use the fleeing
partner to bat them off by guiding the droid to them. If you
get caught, you'll be thrown into the healing spring and be
unable to leave until your partner relieves you, or you both
get caught--at which point, you'll both be transported back to
your base with a three-second stun effect. Use your spy skills
to grab the most jewels before time expires.

Circus Poke Us
Map: Wrinkle Park
Who makes working bumper cars out of glass? This elderly
ringleader, who has instructed that you avoid colliding with
anything so the vehicles don't shatter. The first few seconds
will stick to elements inside the ring, beginning with having
the bumpers shoot up an inch to expand their hidden
umbrella compartments, then come crashing down. At five
seconds, an off-screen net will drop three medium-sized balls,
which will musically bounce around the arena. At twelve
seconds, clowns will enter the arena and perform their sub-
par juggling act, causing several balls to roll around the arena.
At thirty seconds, prepare for oversized peanuts to be lobbed
from the crowd at all angles. At forty-five seconds, the
ringleader will toss in a mix of spinning fire rings, spiked balls
and bowling pins. Watch for the shadows as items are thrown
in, then bait your opponent into retreating a few inches away
by inching closer to them in a move for confusion.

Gadget Go Round
Map: Badge-Wit Centre
Use the gravity control stations to send everyone in a given direction, with the goal of forcing rivals to land on a hole in the cube that leads out into space. Doing so will bar you from using that particular station again for at least five seconds. As the game progresses, more tiles will be exposed, making it a race of survival to be the last player inside the cube as it crumbles.

Special, Deliver Me
Map: Resentment Harbor
The tyrannical T.H.I.S factory owner has gone berserk with admiration over his new invention which will make the delivery system a thousand times more efficient... and he expects you to quicken your sorting pace. While controlling forklifts, one player gets the loads of T.H.I.S. as they fall from dispensers and brings them to their station. Their partner enters button combinations to package loads for the shipping department, earning points for each one sent. If loads stack too high at the receiving zone, you'll be forced to shut down operations for five seconds while you get reprimanded by the factory owner. It's a good strategy for the one manning the forklift to get five loads of T.H.I.S. before making the trip. Teams can only have five loads of T.H.I.S. at one time, so you won't be able to pick up more with the forklift until your station is clear. The only way to slow down the system is by pushing the special button you were told never to touch, which will cease movement for about three seconds. Note that this can only be used once per team before he'll call a technician to check up on the allegedly malfunctioning device.

Space Hatchet
Map: Proper Town
Cameras are rolling on the space-themed set and someone
accidentally left the gravity changer on, causing everyone to
float. Dodge props while you swim in the air and grab axes
that float by, which you can then use to swing at fake meteors
for points. Getting hit by a meteor will cost you five points;
getting hit by an entire planet will both take you back twenty
points and stun you. Satellites can be grabbed and thrown in
the direction of rivals – plan carefully and you can cause a
nasty collision.

Chicken Done
Map: Commuter Terminal
There's always time to earn more cool points, even in life-
threatening situations. The space elevator is collapsing and
you all need to skydive to safety. However, the longer you
wait before the collapsing effect catches up to you, the more
cool points you'll earn. Aim to jump at the very last second.
Problem is, because of the way the camera is situated, you'll
only have a split-second to make the call. So if you start to get
cold feet, it's better to cut your losses before you wind up with
nothing--not even your parachute can help you then.

For All of Time

Map: City of Extinguished Fame

Prevent the elusive flame from surviving long enough to turn the future into an empty abyss. With everyone starting in the ruined city, locate the portals to the past or the present and leap through in pursuit of the enigma. Note that only the present features what you need to defeat the flame: an enlarged reed. The flame only stays in a timeline for five seconds before switching, so either make camp or be quick at portal jumping. At every ten-second mark, shadows with green eyes will universally appear on the ground in all timelines to stun and banish you to the future five seconds later, but you can avoid it by leaving the current timeline. If you're already in the future when they appear, you'll need to teleport out or risk being permanently captured.

#

That wraps up the first part of our guide! Come back next issue for the second part, where we'll cover the twenty-one game boards and all their super-secret matrixes, index cards and hideouts. Yes, twenty-one. Till then, keep your hand dealt-with and those cards shuffled.

Excerpt from a Walkthrough of Bubba Van Helsing, Southern Goth II: South of the Border
By Brandon Barrows

Part VI
Level 4 – Rumble in the Jungle
Overview:
First of all, this is sort of an optional level, but only if you chose not to fight El Sucko, the Chupacabra Lord, back in Stage 3, Apocalyptopulco Beach. If you fight the C.L, you'll wind up heading to Level 5, My Oh Mayan, after a short, power-up-filled bonus level where you can drink mojitos to your heart's content and play grab-ass with the waitresses to boot. It's a pretty sweet alternative to level 4, if you're skilled enough to take down the C.L.

If you do choose instead to fight the much-easier (but also more fun, in my opinion) La Llorona in level 3, you'll end up in the jungle. There isn't a ton of treasure or health-items, but it's a great place to pick up a few extra Tequila Bombs if you're efficient in taking out enemies as you move through the level. Be warned, though! There are a lot of flying enemies that you'll need to either use your Bike Chain to ensnare, ground and Curb Stomp or take very careful aim with Bubba's Scattergun to just blast them out of the sky, as there's not very much ammo in the next couple levels and you don't want to waste any. Basically, every shot counts from here on out, so I recommend saving the gun for when you have no other choice.

Step by Step Walkthrough:

When you appear on the first screen, it looks clear, but stay put for a moment, as a Demonic Cockatoo will swoop out of the upper canopy, shrieking unpleasant things about your not-so-convoluted family tree. If you pay attention, though, you'll see glowing red eyes in the upper part of the screen where the "foliage" starts about a second or two before the D.C. swoops down and be able to avoid the critter without much hassle. This is a good place to practice snagging them with the Bike Chain, too, because you'll have to do a lot of it here – not that you'll mind if you're any sort of real Southern Goth. They may just be evil-infused birds, but who doesn't love stomping down their digital size elevens and being rewarded with the sight of flying eyeballs? Kinda makes me hungry, in fact. Anyway, make very sure that you kill each one as they appear, because you can technically run by them after their first swoop, but they'll follow you, out of sight, up in the canopy until they see a chance to rain feathered havoc down on you and you do not want to have to fight more than one at a time. Individually, they don't do a ton of damage, but if you get two or more onscreen at once, they'll coordinate attacks and make your life a living hell. Well, a bigger hell than being a redneck monster-hunter already is, at any rate, but hey, you chose this life, right?

On the third screen, you'll see your first Hell-Monkey. Pretty sweet, right? I love the little glowing horns and the pentagram tattoo on the chest is a great touch. These aren't too tough by themselves — they just sit there tossing Poop Bombs regardless of what you do — but take them out as soon as possible because on most screens with a H.M., a Demonic Cockatoo will generally show up right after the H.M.'s second bomb. If you slaughter the monkey before the second bomb gets off, though, you'll have no trouble taking the D.C. down on most screens. Your best bet, then, is to let the H.M. toss its first bomb, run forward towards the bomb's arc, duck at the apex of its flight and tap the monkey with your weapon of choice. Simple!

On the fourth screen, there's a H.M. up on the edge of ledge, which makes this a little tricky if you don't immediately run forward when the screen pops because he'll throw a Poop Bomb the second you zone into this area. There's also a Cadejo Malo (my Spanish is rusty, but I think it means "bad dog" or something like that) running back and forth up on the other side of the ledge and after the zone-in, there's nowhere to go but up, so like I said, rush in, swinging that Bike Chain, or the Bubbarang if you found the hidden room on Level 2, to take out the H.M. and make it to the top all in a single leap. Be careful to stay on the very edge of the ledge, though, to avoid running into the C.M. They won't go outside of their programmed "patrol" range, but a single touch will do a lot of damage to your health at this stage of the game – about a third of your whole life bar. It may be tempting to try and avoid the C.D.s when you see them, but do not try to jump over them. The trick with the C.M. is that they jump directly up and slam into you if you do. It kinda looks like they're head-butting your nuts; sort of a doggy vengeance for all their neutered brethren. To kill them, just stay in place outside of their range and attack when they gets close. Three or four swings of the Bike Chain should take it out or a good Scattergun blast, if you feel you have some ammo to spare (not recommended, though). Once the baddies are dead but before you leave this screen, we can get the first of the Tequila Bomb clusters (three bombs per regular-sized cluster). Make sure you have the Bike Chain equipped, then go to the second tree from the right (near the middle of the C.M.'s path), crouch down and then, while still crouching, simultaneously hit the jump button AND the attack button to open up the secret cache in the tree. It's extremely important you have the B.C. equipped, though, because for some reason, in my experience, it only works with that weapon and if you try with any other, you lose your chance. I've heard from some people that it also works with the Bubbarang, but like they say, screenshots or it didn't happen.

The next screen is pretty much smooth sailing, if you've gotten this far and have been paying attention. There's a D.M. right near the screen entrance and between the two tree-stumps a C.M., but you shouldn't have trouble with either. On the sixth screen, you'll need to jump across four stumps of uneven heights and this can be a pain because there's a H.M. on the last stump, a D.C. who appears halfway through and, if you don't take the D.C. out on its first swoop, it'll be joined by a new monster type, the Xavier Cougar who rushes across the screen, doing a weird little, fast-paced salsa-style dance, and will knock you off of your stump. They're a real pain if you don't have split-second reflexes, but I do kind of dig the sound effect that accompanies them, like a burst of some sort of Latin jazz. Anyway, timing and good jump-aim is critical here. I'd strongly recommend equipping the Bubbarang before you leave the last screen, too. When the sixth screen loads, run forward and jump onto the first stump and immediately hit attack to toss your Bubbarang at the H.M. You'll probably take a hit from its Poop Bomb, but fortunately the first stump is wide enough that you shouldn't get knocked off and the slight to moderate damage is worth it, trust me. Leap onto the next stump and pause a second for the D.C. to swoop down, then pop it off with your weapon of choice. If you miss it or whatever, be prepared to leap up as soon as you realize it isn't dead, because the X.C. is so fast you'll have no chance to avoid it once you've seen it. If you do kill the birdie, though, you're pretty much home-free on this screen. Seventh screen, you get a breather – no monsters and if you jump up onto the branch of the fourth tree, you'll find the invisible second Tequila Bomb cluster (regular-sized, so three more bombs). You are, however, presented with a choice of paths: to jump up onto the higher level or continue along at ground level. They both lead to the same place, the final boss battle, but each has pros and cons.

The upper level is long, another whole six screens, and is more of the same stuff you've gotten familiar with by now: Hell Monkeys, Demonic Cockatoos, Cadejo Malos. No Xavier Cougars, though, which is nice, but also no items or treasure of any sort. If you choose this path, you should have no problem making it on your own without my help.

The lower level is much shorter — only three screens — but A) since it's a cave, the roof is low and there isn't much room to maneuver and B) is pretty much filled with C.Ms, H.M.s, yet another a new monster — a spider-type that drops down from the ceiling and, bizarrely, has no name, or even a listing, in the game manual — and X.C.s who dance through at irregular intervals. You're definitely going to take damage going this path, but the monsters here also have a high drop-rate on health items and treasure and, you have a chance at getting the last Tequila Bomb cluster (a big one, giving you five bombs instead of the normal three). So, if you choose this path, my advice is this: clear the first screen of the three H.M.s and the single C.M. with one of your precious Tequila Bombs (since we've already gotten so many, with more to come), then wait until the two spiders drop from the ceiling. If you're lucky, you can take both out with one shot from the Bubbarang. The spiders have very little health, so they're easy to kill, but they inflict a poison effect that there's no way to remove, so keep your distance. The poison will take about fifteen percent of your health, steadily ticking down a percentage point at a time, so avoid contact. Once you kill those spiders off, the first X.C. will probably be dancing through about then if it hasn't already. He'll come from the left side of the screen, instead of the right like in other areas, so just plant yourself on the far right and face back the way you came. I'd recommend actually using your Scattergun here, since you've got plenty of room for once and if you hit it the instant you see the X.C. appear, you should get it in one blast. Like I said, there's no set time period, but he will come and if you don't kill him here, you could very well end up with two on the next screen. Getting caught between two X.C.s is absolutely, positively death. Once you've gotten the X.C. out of the way, head to the next screen, and take a deep breath. You'll see that each of the five little mini-ledges (rock versions of the stumps you crossed earlier) has a H.M. on it, with a C.M. on the bigger ledge on the far side of the screen and, if you wait a second or two, you'll see spiders lowering down into the spaces between each ledge. Adding to that, a X.C. could run through at any time so you've got a big pile on your plate, huh, Bubba? Well, it's not as bad as it looks if you've been carefully marshalling your resources up to this point. Start by waiting until the first spider lowers down so he's face to face with the first H.M., then let loose with the Scattergun or the Bubbarang. I'd recommend the gun because you should be able to take both out with one shot, whereas the 'rang will probably need a couple hits on each monster to kill them and time is of the essence. Once that's done, jump onto the now-clear first mini-ledge and wait about three seconds for the two spiders (the one immediately to your right and the one on the right of the next ledge) drop down, while avoiding the next Poop Bombs from the next H.M., and toss one of your precious Tequila Bombs directly onto the H.M. further to the right. This is important! It has to be precisely timed to the right moment, when both spiders are level with the H.M., and the bomb must be thrown directly onto the monkey to ensure you take out all three at once. There's no other safe, timely way to cross this particular ledge. Now that you've taken out the next two spiders, though, the third ledge should be relatively easy. Just avoid the Poop Bombs and take out the monkey with a couple quick tosses of the Bubbarang, or the Bike Chain if you feel comfortable getting in that close. Repeat the process on the other side to take out the last H.M. and the last of the spiders, then pick off the C.M. any way you please; there's just barely enough room to stand on the edge of its ledge without getting hit. At some point during all of this, a X.C. will show up from the right side of the screen and you'll have to do some fancy footwork to avoid it. Unfortunately, there's no best way to do it so just do whatever works for you. You may end up taking some damage from it, but the C.M. should drop a health item (or at least some treasure, if not). Finally, on the last screen of this path, it looks like you're in the free and clear, but don't get cocky! It appears to be the exit of the cave system, but when you get to the middle of the screen, two X.C.s will rush you from either side of the screen. These are the only X.C.s in the level that are not on a timer as far as I can tell, and their sole purpose is to trick you once you've been lulled into a false sense of security so they'll appear when you reach a specific point on the floor. They aren't as bad as in other areas, though, because there's no pits or other monsters, so just leap straight up as soon as you hit the center of the room and they should rush right underneath you. If you're feeling brave, though, you can pick up the last Tequila Bomb cluster by taking out both X.C.s at once. It took me several tries to get this right, but you have to use another of your Tequila Bombs and basically crouch and leap as you hit the center of the room and hit attack all at the same time so that the T.B. is thrown downwards. If your timing is perfect, it'll blow both X.C.s up and open up a cache in the wall with the bombs. If your timing is off, though, you can get caught in your own blast, so be sure you know what you're doing. The programmers were tricky here, too, because if you avoid the X.C.s and then try to blow up the wall, nothing happens. If you didn't have many T.B.s coming into this level and are confident of your abilities, this is an awesome way to max out your own bomb stash, which will be helpful next level. If you feel comfortable with your supplies, though, it might not be worth risking. Up to you.

And now, except for the boss, we're all done here.

Boss – El Vampiro:

I don't know why an eight-foot tall supposedly-vampiric luchador is out in the middle of the jungle, in broad daylight, no less, but I love that he is. He's definitely one of my favorite bosses in the game in terms of looks and I like to put on my own luchador mask for kicks when I fight him. As far as the battle with El Vampiro itself goes, he's not too bad if you're well-equipped.

First, Tequila Bombs are completely useless against him. He's immune, so don't bother wasting any. You'll also want to get in close for this fight, unlike most other bosses, because if you get too far away, he starts in with some flying wrestling moves, like the flying calf-kick, the leaping neck-breaker and (my favorite of his animations) a big ol' flying belly flop. Consider how huge he is and then think about how much damage that one does! But if you stay in close, within arm's reach, he'll mostly stick to punches, claw-swipes, flipping you the bird and a move where he screeches at you and bats fly out of his mouth. The absolute best weapon to fight him with is the Silver Knucks, which you picked up back in level 2 (if you made your way up to the optional fifth floor of the hotel) and were probably wondering what the heck good they were. The damage on them is admittedly very low, but they have special properties against the undead and especially this guy. For every solid punch you get in, because of the silver, El Vampiro will be stunned for a second or two! Noice, as Bubba's people say!

So your strategy here is to get in close right at the start of the fight before he can launch off any flying moves and just punch away, crouching or leaping to avoid any attacks you can't stun. The one exception is his weird bat-shooting/shrieking thing – it can't be stunned as far as I can tell and crouching doesn't get you low enough to avoid the bats. Pay attention to his facial expressions, because his eyes with flash for a split second and his mouth will start to open really wide just before he does the move. It's pretty obvious once you've seen it the first time and with fair warning, you can either leap over him, which is tough since he's so big, but not impossible since he leans forward a bit to shoot the bats, or you can run back a bit which will give you room to leap over the bats themselves. If you run, just be careful to get back in close quickly before he starts in with the flying attacks.

All in all, this should be a fun, not too hard boss and once you're done, you'll be whisked off to level 5, the previously-mentioned My Oh Mayan.

Level Grade:

Challenge: B

Layout: B-

Graphics: B+

Boss: A- (for fun-level and design alone!)

INTRODUCTORY WALKTHROUGH:
The Chilled Bourbon of Axo-Korvast
By Robin Wyatt Dunn

Level 1

Mom is home after a long visit AWAY. Just ignore her for the
first five minutes, she wants to tell you about AWAY and
what it was like, but if you listen too close it'll confuse you, so
just build your health by doing some jumping jacks, eating the
available fruit, and taking note of all sharp objects in the
kitchen; you're going to need to grab them soon.

As will soon become clear, AWAY is a very bad place, and
Mom now wants to kill herself. If you've done enough
jumping jacks, even though your mother is a very big woman,
you should be able to pin her wrist to the counter and slam
the butcher knife she grabs out of her grip. Then punch her in
the solar plexus to ground her for long enough for you to grab
other nearby sharps and toss them out the kitchen window.

If you don't manage to pin her in time and she opens an
artery, you'll probably have to start over, unless you can
manage to jump onto her shoulders and hold the washcloth
hard onto her neck long enough for it to clot. I've never
managed to pull off that trick, but maybe your finger-skills are
better.

Either way, once she's incapacitated (it's okay to punch her in
the face a few times; you can't kill her), you need to
immediately shut all windows in the house as the voice in
your head is telling you to do. Take note of this particular
voice. Even though it sounds evil, it's good. The good
sounding voice you'll meet later on, on the other hand, is evil.
Very Manichean, right?

As the evil-sounding voice explains, Mom has summoned the
Exat-Katchults from their Extra-Sensory Dimension as a side
effect of her trip AWAY.

To avoid the destruction of your home—the holy vessel acting as a containment field in your home universe—you need to battle off this demonic possession.

If you've sealed all the windows and doors in time, you should have time to remove all your clothing and tie yourself to your own bed. It's much easier to fight demons when you're tied up in bed, believe it or not.

The possession starts when the walls start turning into claws. There's two strategies here. For the first, I'll assume you've successfully tied yourself to your bed before shit goes haywire.

Level 1A: Possession in Bed

Just like the little girl in Exorcist, you're going to be doing some nasty shit, to wit: projectile vomiting. Unlike the green projectile puke in the movie, this puke can melt walls and summon interdimensional demon portals, so the trick is to cover the walls of your room evenly in your own puke. Don't concentrate on any one area, this is the way you lose. (And you don't want to lose because the corporate sponsors of the game have some nasty financial side effects in store for you . . . just warning you. You didn't think playing games was safe, did you?)

As you'll probably figure out, the demon-spawn can simply be destroyed with a direct projectile-puke, unless you're playing on expert difficulty, in which case it'll take both a projectile-puke, and then you'll have to wait till it jumps for your neck, and you'll have to grab it in your teeth and shake it till it's dead. (You'll get the hang of it).

Once you've killed about twenty of them, it's safe to untie yourself and go on to Level 2.

Level 1B: Possession, NOT in Bed

Okay, so you failed to take the easy way. The causative logic of The Chilled Bourbon of Axo-Korvast often revolves around opposites: the weaker you can make yourself appear, the easier it will be to beat back Evil. Look too strong, and you'll have the Devil's time of it.

What this means is a Big Demon Spawn is going to launch through your ceiling any minute: there he is, looking sort of like Shrek with more teeth. Remember: no weapons! If you try that he'll kill you more or less instantly.

Once again, you have to go at him with your own dumb human teeth. Good luck!

Level 2:

The Wine Cellar

Some critics have claimed that the money behind this game has some kind of retro-Prohibition value system, and the reason that the Evil concentrates around the wine cellar is that ALCOHOL IS SATAN or something. I don't know, I don't have the kind of time those critics have. Anyway, it's funny as hell!

Having defeated the first demon infestation, you must now kill your mother. Don't worry, she'll come back to life! As the evil voice in your head explains, if she took her own life then she'd be possessed by evil demons, whereas if you, Avatar of the Light, kill her, she'll be possessed by good demons. Believe me, you'll be able to tell the difference.

Have fun killing her; but not too much fun! The game punishes sheer sadism.

So now head into the cellar! And open up one of those kegs and start sucking on it! You need to be as drunk as possible! (It's actually faster, if you have time, to put your fingers down your throat and induce vomiting before you glue your lips to the keg, in terms of alcohol-absorption rate).

Since this is "Satanic" wine, it won't just make you drunk, it will put you in touch with the Demons from AWAY.

As the room turns red and you grow claws, try to pinpoint through your fogged vision the Portal Positions – your map will be unreliable and you'll have to use dead-reckoning to hack and slash your way towards them.

Paradoxically, as you kill this round of demons (watch out for the brain-sucking ones!), you need to avoid spilling more wine, because, unless it's in your stomach, it's just going to summon more demons.

The principle of closing interdimensional demon portals is simple: shout as loud as possible, using the demon words you hear in your head. The part of me that wishes (please let that part of me atrophy this year!) I could have been a game designer wants to know how they programmed the audio-recognition logic to track the emotional valences in your voice as you shout out the demon incantations into the Hell-Holes, but I guess there's government technology for that stuff, and what not.

Anyway, shout the hell out of them, listen to the evil voice, and you should be okay. I actually managed to shut one of them down while a demon was sucking out my brains, and since that demon had spawned from that particular portal, it died when the portal closed (although then I had to finish the level with the use of only one arm; the other had gone dead). If you successfully close all three or four portals before your house is destroyed, your mother will re-animate and you can begin the next narrative sequence where she explains how to find the eponymous Bourbon that will permit your own passage AWAY.

Remember, don't play too late at night, and don't use your mom's credit card!

GOBBLE AND GO!
By Fred Schiller

In the beginning there was darkness, cold, hunger, and sticky puddles of leftover primordial ooze which, if stepped into, would turn your feet black and cause them to give off the smell of rotting feet.

Thousands of years passed and things had improved a bit. We had the incandescent light bulb to see by, Sears Kenmore furnaces for heat, galoshes to help put an end to rotten foot disease, and to curb hunger we had hundreds and hundreds of fast food drive-through restaurants.

The "Route 66 GOBBLE AND GO Cross Country Rally" combines three of Americans' favorite activities: driving like crazy, being exploited by network TV game shows, and eating enough fast food quickly enough to overload even the most robust heart-pacemaker.

Players start the game behind the wheel of a 1974 ROADBLASTER DELUXE and as they pile on the miles (and the pounds) they can upgrade the tires, engine, suspension, and customize their ride with nitrous oxide, machine gun turrets, and roof-mounted missiles.

Contestants vie for prize money and deep-fried rewards driving from Santa Monica, CA to Chicago, IL along Route 66. The famous Route 66 might not be the fastest way to travel from Los Angeles to Chicago, but it does offer rally contestants a seemingly endless menu of deep-fried, cheese-stuffed, barbecue-sauce-drenched, curry-coated entrees.

In this game, the only thing more important than your driving speed is your caloric intake. If your Roadblaster Deluxe can't do more than 20 m.p.h. up hills and grades, that's understandable and will be tolerated. But if your caloric intake drops below 35,000 units a day, you could face disqualification.

To identify Restaurants, Tourist Traps, Gas Stations, and Drive-Through Snack Shacks that are participating in the road rally, just look for the EMERGENCY RACE SERVICES FLAG. Each location displaying this flag is guaranteed to have a mechanic, a sous chef, a renowned heart surgeon, and at least three pastry chefs on staff around the clock.

The biggest threats you'll face in GOBBLE AND GO are the HEALTH NUTZ. They are to fast food aficionados as Greenpeace is to whale hunters. They drive a variety of vehicles that are capable of creating roadblocks, ramming players off the road, or even harpooning the behemoth motor-homes and dragging them to a dead stop. In most cases you can ROCK THE BOAT and eventually free yourself, but if this happens near a SALAD THE HUT restaurant or a HEALTHY HAVEN Health-Food Shoppe, your death is imminent.

Fast Food Restaurants
- Juan & Dawn's Tiny Taco Kingdom
- Billy Ray's Ballistic Burritos
- Off the Leash Dogs
- The Chili Moat
- Fakin' Bacon—Tofu Faux-Pork-on-a-Stick
- Captain Chunky Chicken's Chicken Chunks
- Onion Ring Oasis
- Sly's Fries & Slaw
- Prof. Salty's Fission Chips
- Bucket O' Burgers
- Sgt. Snorkel's Subs
- Drive-Thru Snack Shacks
- Boston Bob's Barn Burnin' Baked Beans
- Shiverin' Steve's Shakes
- Stampede & Mead
- Burger She Wrote
- Pizza My Heart
- We're Not Shellfish with Our Seafood
- Meatloaf—Any Way You Want It!
- Catfish Café

- Do Dive In – Microwaved Seafood Delicacies
- Wizard of Cod
- Not so awful Falafels
- Crusty Dan's Fish Burgers
- Bucket O' Beef
- Tourist Trap Stands
- Sunshine Slurshies
- Aunt Daffy's Saltwater Taffy
- Shesells Seashells & More
- Too Tight T-Shirts
- Auntie's Antique Attic (elevator broken)
- Yogurt Treats & Tile Grout
- Drive-Thru Tattoo
- Familiar Phil's Foot Spa
- Tan in a Minute
- Darnell's Diet Fudge Shack
- In the Dark - Permanent Make-up
- Snacks and More (always out of snacks)
- Tiny's Trampoline Town
- Gas Stations and Garages
- Outstanding Octane
- Phil R. Up's Gasoline
- Motor Home Modification Emporium
- Last Gas (Until the Next One)
- Don't be Fuelish Pit Stoppe (1960s British theme)
- Buster Knuckles' Machine Shop
- Pump n' Jump
- Zoomi Indian Nation Tire Repair
- Tanks a Lot Gas
- Gas & Little Powdered Donuts (Out of donuts)
- Beefsticks, Gas & More
- Fill It To the Brim with Gin (Moonshine Runner motif)

Racing a motorhome can be hard business and the 1980s is a complicated time to live, so if you're having trouble completing "Gobble and Go", help has arrived.

Admitting that you need help can be harder for some people than lifting a heavy rock, but sometimes rocks need to be lifted and people need a little help with a game.

HINTS, TIPS, TRICKS, SHORTCUTS, AND STRATEGY SUGGESTIONS FOR "GOBBLE AND GO"

If you've played for any length of time you know that accidents happen regularly and that filling out reports for the police and getting your Roadblaster Deluxe repaired and back on the road can be a hassle. There is a shortcut that will keep your belly full of artery-clogging delicacies. At each accident scene you'll see ambulances from places like "Suzy Kay's Death on Wheels", "You Bleed and We'll Drive", and former NFL coach "Ripsaw O'Brien's Meat Wagons". Most players will ignore these annoyances but they could be a big help. USE one of the ambulances services and after a kidney-jarring ride to the hospital you'll be quickly treated, fed an epic meal loaded with creamy sauces and all sorts of meats and cheeses. (Don't bother just loosening your belt, you're going to eat so much it's best to just take your pants over before it's too late and you have to cut them off.) After you've tucked away a couple of platters you're ready to go. Your Roadblaster will be waiting outside the hospital with a full tank of fuel and most of the dents pounded out. Regardless of whether you go to the hospital or not, it will take you the same amount of time to get back into the race, so why not fill your belly and your gas tank at the same time?

If you're having some troubles making those hairpin turns on Route 66, or if you can't get the knack of tipping your motorhome over and riding on two wheels to get past blocked roadways, you need to play a few games of "Cactus Dick's Rally Raceway". You'll find the arcade game at dozens of gas stations and restaurants along your gastronomical race down Route 66, but they will all be out of service with the exception of the units at Burger She Wrote, Tiny's Trampoline Town, and Buster Knuckles' Machine Shop. After a quick puzzle of putting the correct number of tokens in the correct slots, Cactus Dick himself appears in the rear-view game-screen, recommending you buckle up because it's gonna be a bumpy as hell ride. Sparks and electrical sputtering happen in and out of the game, which has begun to billow smoke. You start driving, but if you miss enough simple tasks in this game Cactus Dick himself will take control of the wheel and show you how a manly man drives. Each time he aces a difficult driving maneuver you get a teeth-chattering jolt of electricity that is imbedding the information in your game brain.

Winning a Road Rally is a difficult task even if you have a map to show you, not only the roadway, but all the deep-fried, gravy-soaked, cream-filled food stops. Everyone starts the game with the same map, but they have a way of vanishing or getting coated with birtchbark taffy so it's unreadable. Salvation lies in the ladies rooms of all the Boston Bob's Barn Burnin' Baked Beans Shack. Mounted onto the wall in the sittin' stall is a detailed road map for the "Gobble n' Go: Routs 66 Cross town Rally". Don't waste your time trying to yank the map off the wall. The simple but annoying trick is to use a nasty old lipstick you find on the floor with a paper toilet-seat to draw the map. It takes a few minutes, but if you succeed not only will you have a nearly perfect recreation of your map, but it will list new or not as popular locations on your original. (So you'll get locations that people who just draw their own version of the map at home won't be privy to.) This can be a little frustrating because female customers from Boston Bob's Barn Burnin' Baked Beans Shack will occasionally need to use the restroom, and by the time you get back in there, your map will be a soggy mess on the floor and you'll need to start all over again.

Many of the rest-stop and touristy traps are run by the Zoomi Indian Nation. Along your path you may need tires and the Zoomi Indian Nation Tire Repair is full of good people. If instead of dumping all your tokens into the arcade games, you give one to the little Zoomi girl standing near the air hose, she'll sing you a little song. If you make it all the way through the song she'll give you a rock, which is an invitation to a Zoomi Campfire Gathering. After a questionable feast of stuffed scorpion carcass, pig-fly pie, and tortoise quencher served right from the tortoise, you start getting woozy from the smell of burning tires, and whatever was in that tortoise quencher, and soon pass out.

You wake on the simmering summer plains of a vision quest. You'll wander through the drifting deserts and meet characters you've interacted with before, plus some new one-offs who only speak in Esperanto. Phil from Familiar Phil's Foot Spa will seek you out and he at least speaks English to you. If you promise him your soul on weekends and holidays in the next life, he will take you on a journey. You travel to an abandoned Crusty Dan's Fish Burgers location that is almost buried in the sand. Inside, you see a rusted fork on the lunch counter. The fork slowly twists back and forth in place like the compass of a ship at sea. After this point, the first Crusty Dan's Fish Burgers restaurant you visit will have that rusted fork stuck to the counter. If you bring the fork outside and set it on the road it will eventually point to an overgrown bit of shrubbery or a dilapidated building. Driving in the direction the fork points will cause you to jump ahead in the race.

We hope you had a good time playing "Route 66 Gobble and Go: Cross Country Rally". The thought that our forefathers fought through all sorts of adversity and foot fungus in ensure our freedom to eat what we want, and where and when we want it, brings a tear of joy to my eye. Driving fast to get unhealthy food is as American as being on COPS for the first time, or deep-frying a turkey and having the whole pot of oil catch fire and burn like Satan's hemorrhoids. We hope you'll come back and play again and again. You could probably play a hundred times and still never find all the sweet secrets hiding along Route 66. To perfectly honest, most of the designers and programmers were under the influence of something called "purple drank" and they have no idea of what weird and twisted things could be lurking in the furthest corners of the game. If players come across hidden areas full of weird activities be sure to write to us care of the internet. Thanks again for playing. You're all winners in our book -- if that makes you feel any better.